Thomas Sedgwick Whalley

The Castle of Montval

Thomas Sedgwick Whalley

The Castle of Montval

ISBN/EAN: 9783743390621

Manufactured in Europe, USA, Canada, Australia, Japa

Cover: Foto ©Andreas Hilbeck / pixelio.de

Manufactured and distributed by brebook publishing software
(www.brebook.com)

Thomas Sedgwick Whalley

The Castle of Montval

THE

CASTLE OF MONTVAL,

A TRAGEDY,

IN FIVE ACTS,

AS IT IS NOW PERFORMING

WITH UNIVERSAL APPLAUSE

AT THE

THEATRE ROYAL DRURY LANE,

By the Rev. T. S. WHALLEY.

Second Edition.

L O N D O N:

PRINTED FOR R. PHILLIPS, NO. 71, ST. PAUL's
CHURCH-YARD.

SOLD BY H. D. SYMONDS, AND T. HURST, PATERNOSTER-ROW;
CARPENTER AND CO. OLD BOND-STREET; AND BY ALL
OTHER BOOKSELLERS.

1799.

TO MRS. SIDDONS.

DEAR MADAM,

As the Caftle of Montval owes its favourable reception by the Public entirely to your matchlefs exertions, its dedication to you would be a debt of gratitude, were it not one of friendfhip. If the audience has been enchanted with your performance of a part, which was written folely for *you*, what muft the Author's fenfations have been, who felt that the zeal of the friend gave an higher tone and colouring to the enthufiafms of the actrefs.

I prefume not to divide the palm with you, but when wreathed round your brow, I *may* be proud that its graceful honours owe some-

b   thing

thing to a Drama, which you infpired, and which, through you, will afford lafting fatif-faction to,

Dear Madam,

Your obliged and faithful Friend, &c. &c.

THO⁵. S. WHALLEY.

PREFACE.

THE following tragedy is founded on a well-known fact, which happened, the author believes, somewhere in the South of France, and so recently as in the year Eighty-three. The old count in question, had been immured in a secret dungeon six years, by his cruel son, and a confidential villian who had been bred up in the castle, when he was accidentally discovered by a nobleman who was the old count's particular friend. Not having heard of the count's supposed death (owing to a long absence from France), he unexpectedly arrived to pass a few days with him, when the castle was so full of guests, that the old count's bed-chamber was the only one unoccupied. This chamber communicated with the dungeon by a secret door, concealed by tapestry; and through the hurry attending the revelry in the castle, had been left open by the young count's abominable agent, the evening his father's old friend was to sleep in a room which had been carefully shut up till that night, ever since the count's supposed decease. In the course of

b 2   the

the night, the noble gueſt, awakened by a noiſe in the chamber, diſcovered his old friend, and an explanation taking place, the officers of juſtice were, unexpectedly, called in the next day from a neighbouring city: the old count was liberated, but, too feeble to bear ſuch a ſudden change, died in a few days; his execrable ſon was condemned to be impriſoned for his life, which would not have been ſpared, but at the powerful interceſſion of his noble relations, who, according to the laws of France, would have been diſgraced and degraded by his public and merited execution. The part of the counteſs, with ſome others, have been imagined by the author, to form a plot fit for the ſtage; and to give it all the advantages of Mrs. Siddons's unrivalled performance. How well ſhe has juſtified his hopes, the public, whom ſhe has enchanted with her tranſcendent efforts, knows; but it cannot know how much ſhe has ſurpaſſed his higheſt expectations in a part, which, as it was only written for her, ſo ſhe only could have given it ſuch wonderful force and effect.

It has been ſuppoſed by ſome, that the author borrowed his plot partly from the Robbers, and partly from the Caſtle Spectre. The plain and honeſt narrative he has given will, he truſts, vindicate him from this imagined

gined

gined imitation. Indeed his tragedy was written fome
time before he read the play of the Robbers, and as
it was in the hands of the managers of Drury-lane
Theatre very early in May 1797, no part of it could
have been ftolen from the Caftle Spectre, which was
put into their hands fome time after, and which ought,
in juftice, to have fucceeded, and not preceded, the
Caftle of Montval on the ftage.

The AUTHOR.

PROLOGUE BY THE AUTHOR.

Spoken by Mr. POWELL.

A TRAGEDY again?—Aye, he may try,
With dagger, ftrut, and rant, to make us cry;
But all his efforts, and his kill, kill, kill!
Shall never make us weep againft our will:
We love to laugh!—then, pray, why here to night?
Can it be out of whim, or out of fpight?
I'll not believe it; Britons are too kind,
Too generous, to betray a grov'ling mind!
Some critic fly, or poet in a corner,
May, here and there, perhaps, perform the fcorner
And come refolv'd to damn: fince wits, they fay,
Like hungry wolves, for want of other prey,
On their own kind will turn; and thro' the town,
To gaol from garret, hunt each other down.
But yet—tho' authors are fo hard of heart---
Ye, gentle fair, will act a gentler part;
And have your falts and handkerchiefs prepar'd
For tears, which are the poet's beft reward.
And fympathetic beaux can't fail to cry
At your command, and utter figh for figh.
From you, O gallery gods! there's nought to fear,
If genuine pathos calls the genuine tear:
Nor will the judgment of the pit refufe
Enlighten'd plaudits to the tragic mufe,
If Nature, leagu'd with Pity, plays her part,
To agitate the pulfes of the heart.
Howe'er the author in his part may fail,
Truth has fupply'd the fubject of his tale.

Gallia—

Gallia—where all to mad excefs is borne;
Where ev'ry tie of God and man is torn;
Where fuff'ring virtue lifts her hands in vain,
And cheated freedom drags his iron chain—
Gallia fupply'd the ftory, which, to-night,
With tender fympathy and fad delight,
If hope deceive not, thro' our cares, fhall claim,
And your applaufe, one laurel leaf from fame;
One leaf, if haply one ungather'd grows,
To wreath our naval heroes' gallant brows.

DRAMATIS PERSONÆ.

COUNT *of* MONTVAL,	Mr. HOLLAND.
MARQUIS *of* VAUBLANE,	Mr. C. KEMBLE.
COUNT *of* COLMAR,	Mr. AICKIN.
OLD COUNT,	Mr. KEMBLE.
MONS. LAPONT,	Mr. BARRYMORE.
BLAISE, *the old Steward of the Castle,*	Mr. PACKER.
COUNTESS *of* MONTVAL,	Mrs. SIDDONS.
The LADY MATILDA, *her Cousin,*	Mrs. POWELL.
TERESA, *Woman to the Countess,*	Miss HEARD.

Scene lies in Dauphiny, in the South of France.

THE

CASTLE OF MONTVAL.

SCENE I—*A handsome Antichamber in the Castle.*

Enter TERESA *and* BLAISE, *talking.*

TERESA.

I Cannot think it: sure your former lady
Was far less lovely than my charming mistress!

BLAISE.

It may be so in any eyes but mine.
Train'd, from a boy, by her protecting hand;
Taken from poverty, and rais'd to honor;
Trusted by *her*, and by my noble lord;
My eyes can never see their equals more!
But yet, Teresa, I confess the countess
Reminds me of the beauty now laid low;
And bears such grace and dignity about her,
As I did never think to see again.

TERESA.

Well, worthy Blaise, your gratitude I honor,
Tho' I may doubt your taste.---But the late count ?---

BLAISE.

O! my dear master!---Pray excuse these tears!---
Was goodness, honor, kindness, past my speak-
ing!

TERESA.

When did he die ?

BLAISE.

About four years ago.
His death was fudden ; and a fudden change—
To *me* a fad one, who was wont to think
That all his wifdom order'd was moft right—
Then happen'd here.

TERESA.

What change, my worthy friend?

BLAISE,

Excefs and revelry, for tranquil ftate :
The noonday frolic, and the midnight feaft,
For fober chearfulnefs, and fober hours ;
For hofpitality, whofe even courfe
Flow'd always full, yet never ran to wafte.
But I am old : fafhions and times are alter'd :
I fhou'd not blame, becaufe *I* cannot relifh
What my young lord, impell'd by health and fpirits,
Thinks fit to do —And I've a confidence
That by your lady much will be reform'd
That feem'd amifs.—O ! may his actions honor
His noble parents, and his noble wife !

TERESA.

And fo I truft they *will*: now Heav'n forbid
Such excellence as her's were thrown away.—

BLAISE *(interrupting her)*.

What *have* I faid ?—Young woman do not think
it !
Wreft not my words ; I pray you wreft them not
Beyond their meaning !—He is gay and young,

And

And youth is lavifh, when the tide of fortune
Draws flatt'rers round ; a bafe and bufy train!
But I am wrong again :—we'll hope the beft.
No more ! for fee my lady's noble friends.

[*Exeunt.*

Enter MATILDA *and the* MARQUIS.

MARQUIS.

My dear Matilda, let the precious moments
Which fortune offers, be employ'd to fpeak
My conftant love and overflowing rapture,
At meeting thus again!---At meeting *thus*,
After fo many tedious months of abfence,
With full allowance from your noble father,
To urge my wifhes and exprefs my joy.

MATILDA.

What fhall I anfwer worthy you and me ?
Believe *my heart* refponfive to *your own* ;
Tho' female delicacy makes my tongue
Bafhful to fpeak the language it infpires.

MARQUIS.

Long, *long* I lov'd, without one ray to cheer me !
Then fpare not to enchant a faithful lover,
Whofe thoughts and paffion you, for years, have
known
So fervently devoted to your charms !

MATILDA.

You *know* enough to know what I cou'd fay ;
And feel enough to know what *are* my feelings.
Content with *this*, prefs my fond heart no further !

B 2 But

But tell me, how you like the charming countefs?
Tho' fhort your knowledge, in one tranfient day,
To penetrate the virtues of her heart.

MARQUIS.

Enough that knowledge to difcern her merit.
To fay fhe's worthy my Matilda's friendfhip,
Speaks all that eloquence *cou'd* fay to praife her.

MATILDA.

From longer intimacy you muft learn
Her high perfeftions.—In her noble foul
A graceful fortitude, that dares all trial,
Lives with a tendernefs that's all her own,
Nothing in her, in perfon or in mind,
But greatly excellent, and greatly fair.
Her beauty has a fomething of divine!
A dignity, that fhews all others mean,
Was ever fuch a majefty of eye!
Such bright effulgence blended with fuch foftnefs!
And thus her lofty foul fuperior fhines,
Among the beft and nobleft of her fex!
Attach'd from childhood, and allied by blood,
My admiration ftill acquires new force;
And while I love her *tenderly*, I feel
An awe and wonder, mingled with affeftion!—
But looking *all*, and *more* than *all*, I've faid.——
The lovely countefs comes!

> (*As Matilda is fpeaking, the folding Doors of a
> magnificent Saloon are thrown open, and the
> Count and Countefs, attended by Lapont, ad-
> vance through them to the Front of the Stage.*)

COUNT.

COUNT.

My good Lapont,
I pray you fee that ev'ry thing's in order
For my departure.

LAPONT.

All fhall be prepared,   [*Exit.*

COUNTESS.

Join me, my noble friends, join to perfuade
My deareft lord from quitting this fair manfion!

MATILDA.

Quitting this manfion!---We had fondly hop'd
That many happy weeks wou'd glide away,
Before our friendly party knew divifion!

COUNT.

With grief of heart, alas! I'm forc'd to leave
Thefe tranquil joys for hateful occupations.
Hateful, alike, to friendfhip, and to love!

COUNTESS.

Indeed, Montval, I cannot take it kind
You thus defert me!

COUNT.

Why, my foul's delight,
Why blame what hard neceffity requires?

COUNTESS.

What fudden bufinefs, thus, fhou'd force you back
From thefe calm fhades, to *that detefted Paris?*
The feat of every vice and every crime!
Why cannot letters, or fome trufty agent?---

COUNT.

If it *cou'd* be---if *pers'onal* application,
In the great caufe, you *know*, I have in hand,
Were not demanded---think you I wou'd leave---
" Look at your face reflected from that mirror,"
                                        Then

Then think if I *wou'd* leave thofe heav'nly charms,
For aught of pleafure that the world *can* give !

COUNTESS.

'Tis ever fo !---Money's the *bane* of blifs !---
The bafe alloy of honor, duty, love.

COUNT *(agitated.)*

Why fpeak you *thus ?*——*Has* it corrupted *me ?*—
But I will haften to thy arms again,
And recompence the languifhings of abfence,
On thy dear bofom !——

COUNTESS.

Well ! I am your wife :
A poor weak woman ; doom'd to acquiefce,
By duty, as by nature.——

COUNT.

Take it not fo,
My beft beloved !—*Mine* is the *cruel* tafk,
Whofe only earthy joy is in thy fmiles.
Your charming friend, and her deferving marquis,
Shall foothe your widow'd hours.

MATILDA.

The lovely countefs,
At all times, may command my fervices ;
The willing tribute of my juft devotion.

MARQUIS.

And mine.—And if my pow'r but mate my will,
Your abfence, count, tho' not, perhaps, forgotten,
Shall not awaken fuch fevere regret,
To banifh mirth, and frown the fmiles away.

COUNTESS.

My noble friends, I know your gen'rous hearts,

And

And have a full reliance on your kindnefs.
Well, well! if you *muft* go, I'll do my beft:
To foften folitude till your return.—
The proud anceftral oaks that wave around
This tow'ring caftle fhall affift my mufing.
The awful rocks fhall tempt my wand'ring feet,
To vifit their receffes ; and the torrents
Shall deafen my complaints, as they arife.—
But ere you go, allow, at leaft, the time
To vifit every corner of this manfion ;
Its gloomy grandeur is in unifion
With the fad temper of my penfive mind.

COUNT. *(embarraffed.)*

At my return!——Time preffes——

COUNTESS.

Then old Blaife
Shall be my guide thro' all its labyrinths.

COUNT. *(earneftly.)*

Not fo, my deareft love !—Wait my return!
I pray you wait !—Deny me not this pleafure !

COUNTESS.

Nay, in the abfence of my honor'd lord,
It were a fcrutiny I fhou'd little tafte.

COUNT.

My foul's beft treafure ! take, in this embrace,
My ftock of pleafure, till we meet again !

COUNTESS.

Beware the fyrens of that hateful Paris !
I have a foul that cannot brook a rival,
Nor cou'd defcend to a degenerate hufband.
My love goes only hand in hand with virtue;

And

And tho' my heart fhou'd burft in the attempt,
I'd tear it from the man I cou'd not honor !

COUNT.

Ah ! why this earneftnefs ?—You cannot doubt
me !
By *this !* and *this !* I'm your's——

COUNTESS (embracing him).

My dear Montval !
My heart can know no joy till your return !

[Exit Count.

I'm ftrangely mov'd !

MATILDA.

I pray compofe your fpirits !
Why *fkou'd* you take this journey thus to heart ?
Bufinefs *muft* fometimes interfere with love :
This tranfient abfence will increafe your pleafure,
And zeft affection, when the count returns.

COUNTESS.

O ! my dear friend, my trembling heart affures me,
It is too tender for my lafting peace.——
Wou'd it were calmer !——

MARQUIS.

Say not fo, dear lady !
This fenfibility fo well becomes you,
That it new luftre gives to ev'ry charm.

COUNTESS.

I know your gallantry, and feel your friendfhip.
But weary as my foul was grown of Paris,
And all its giddy round of diffipation,
I can't endure—when, at my *earneft fuit,*
The count was *hardly* won to leave its magic,
And vifit once again—with *me*—his *bride*—

His

His native fhades—I *can't endure* to fee him,
Impatient, thus to hurry back again.—

MARQUIS.

Remember, urgent bufinefs calls him thither,
Of great importance to your future ftate ;
Elfe were he much to blame.—

COUNTESS.

I know it not.
I heard of no exprefs! I faw no letters !
This fudden recollection does not pleafe me.
But two fhort days have I enjoy'd him here
(And thofe have feen him reftlefs, gloomy, abfent !)
I! whofe fond hopes had pictur'd fo much blifs
From this retreat, by *nature* form'd to charm ;
And which to *him*, if *rightly* turn'd his mind,
Shou'd wake a thoufand, thoufand fond ideas,
From time foregone, and fond habitual feelings !

MATILDA.

No doubt the count, with equal pride and pleafure,
Will hafte to join you in his native caftle,
And wander, with the idol of his heart,
Thro' the romantic fcenery around.

MARQUIS.

Believe he will! He cannot be fo cold,
So flow of pulfe, amidft his native fhades,
To feel no fervor, and exprefs no joy :
Far *different* is the *ardor* of his *mind*.

COUNTESS.

You do him friendly juftice—Die the thought
That wou'd debafe him!—But, my noble friend,
Can you inform me *who* is this Lapont ?

C

MARQUIS.

As I have heard, a tenant's orphan fon,
Who fofter'd by the hand of the late count,
Took root within his bofom,
And made, from early youth, the humble friend,
Of your dear lord, now claims that honor'd title.

COUNTESS.

He looks unworthy of fo high a place.
His fair demeanour, and obfequious bendings,
Delight not me.—I like more fimple manners.
Malignant meanings play about his lips;
While, ever and anon, upon his brow,
Bufhy and black, dark fraud and paffions lour,
Spite of his caution to conceal their workings.
How like *you* him ?—

MARQUIS.

In truth I know him not.
Yet, I am free to think, and free to fay,
He never fhou'd have been my chofen friend.

COUNTESS.

Nor fhall be Montval's.—Nothing that's ignoble
Shall win his confidence, or gain his ear,
I can influence. But more of *this*
As time fhall ferve.—To *you*, without referve,
I pour out the emotions of my foul.

Enter BLAISE.

The Count of Colmar, madam, waits your prefence.

COUNTESS.

I come, good Blaife. (*Exit* BLAISE.) But pray inform
me, marquis,
Who *is* this vifitor?

MARQUIS.

MARQUIS.

The chofen friend
Of the late count, and worthy well the title.

COUNTESS.

Then go we to him, for I reverence age,
When dignified with honorable virtues.

[*Exeunt.*

SCENE—*Changes to the great gothic Hall of the Caftle.*

Enter the COUNT *and* LAPONT, *in clofe Conference.*

COUNT.

My good Lapont, remember what I've faid!
You know its confequence.

LAPONT.

Count, do not doubt me!
My ftake is great as *your's.* But now the money.—
I have an urgent purpofe for that fum.

COUNT.

How *can* that be, Lapont? It is not long
Since you receiv'd a liberal fupply.
Retain'd, and almoft mafter in this caftle,
What preffing wants——

LAPONT.

Afk you, my lord, what wants?
Have I not paffions, think you, like your own,
That call, and *loudly* too, for gratification?
Shall I, for ever, eat dependent bread?
Nor while your power with your life remains,
Lay up fome ftore, for my declining years?

C 2 COUNT.

COUNT.

Nay, my good friend, this heat becomes you not!
There is the money; giv'n with free good-will;
Tho', think not, if an earthly tomb awaits me,
That I fhou'd leave thy fortunes deftitute!

LAPONT.

I dare not run the hazard.

COUNT.

Dare not run !——

LAPONT.

Come, come, my lord, we know each other *well* :
But on fuch knowledge grows not *confidence*.
As far as mutual fecrets may affect
Our mutual fafety, we *may truft each other*.

COUNT.

" The villain!" *(afide)* Well, Lapont, no more of this.
What *have* I done to waken fuch fufpicion?
My gen'rous kindnefs merits better thoughts.——
But I muft go.—This houfe to *me* is *hateful*,
Tho' it contains the object I adore.——

LAPONT.

Why did you come, then, if your timid heart,
Relax'd of nerve, ftarts at its own emotions,
And dares to *do*, what it not dares to think of?
Have you *quite* loft the firmnefs of your temper?

COUNT.

I fcorn my abject foul, yet can't command it;
Deride its childifh fears, yet feel them ftill:
Abfent from hence, I never know thefe terrors;
Nor *here fhou'd* know them, if but one event—
You guefs my meaning—fet my heart at reft.

LAPONT.

LAPONT.

'Tis marvellous it happen'd not long fince!
But it *muft* happen *foon*.   Why, then, meanwhile,
Why came you hither, to difturb your peace,
And wake the fleeping torment in your bofom?

COUNT.

The countefs, whom I worfhip—for did ever
Such grace and beauty meet thy dazzled eyes?—
The *countefs* wou'd not be denied this boon.
Romantic, ardent, vifionary, fond,
She figh'd to quit the gay and fplendid world,
And wander with me, thro' my native fhades;
Seeing her bent, paft hope, to quit the court,
I prefs'd a vifit to the duke her father,
And feign'd a ftrong defire to fee his caftle,
Fam'd for its grandeur, and its wide domain.

LAPONT.

Feign'd a *defire*, where you may well *command?*
What, does a woman govern thus your reafon,
And lead her puppet as her fancy leads?
For fhame! for fhame!—remember you're a *man!*

COUNT.

Form'd to command, and captivate all hearts,
I own, her talents, aided by her charms,
Make me a ready flave to all her wifhes:
What once has got poffeffion of her mind,
She follows with fuch fervency of paffion,
As cannot brook controul.—Here, then, fhe *is*;
But here, tho' fick at heart, to tear me from her,
The world fhou'd not induce my longer ftay!

She

She foon fhall follow me :—I will contrive
To draw her back, by fome pretence, to *Paris*.
While fhe is *here*, I fhall not know repofe.
There are the *keys*; and never may *thefe hands*
Feel their *cold touch*, or know *their office* more !

> [*Throws down a bunch of keys on a table, and exit*
> *haftily;* LAPONT *as haftily following and calling*
> *after him, leaving the keys behind—*

Stay, count !—I muft intreat fome private converfe,
On matters of great moment, ere we part !—

END OF THE FIRST ACT.

ACT II.

SCENE I.

A magnificent Apartment, where the COUNTESS,
the MARQUIS, *the* COUNT OF COLMAR, *and*
MATILDA, *appear conversing.*

COUNTESS.

I LOVE to hear these tales of former days,
Which move the mind to useful retrospection,
And seem to give it new and longer being.—.
Your rev'rence for my Albert's noble father,
Delights my soul.—Your zeal proclaims his worth.

COUNT OF COLMAR.

It was transcendent! For his noble mind,
Gen'rous as kind, to all around diffus'd
Unnumber'd blessings!—To the rich, and poor,
His gates and hand and heart were ever open,
With courteous dignity, and temper'd state;
That mix'd with liberal plenty, wise expence;
Invited ease, and yet inspir'd respect;
Allur'd to mirth, yet banish'd noisy riot.
He *was*, what great men *shou'd* be; what, alas!
I *knew*, but never hope to know again!—

COUNTESS.

COUNTESS.

I wonder, Montval, with the nat'ral pride
A fon *fhou'd* feel, offspring of fuch a father!—
I wonder that his tongue fhou'd not be lavifh
On fuch a theme!—If I am not miftaken,
He loft his noble mother when a child.

COUNT.

He *did:* and great the lofs! for ne'er was beauty
Inform'd with clearer fenfe, or fweeter temper,
Or deck'd and dignified by higher virtue.

COUNTESS.

I fhou'd not grieve that fhe has long been dead:
My poor deferts wou'd but have been a foil
To her endowments.

COLMAR.

O that fhe *had* liv'd,
She and the count, to fee their only fon
Mated, with beauty, fortune, virtue, birth,
Beyond their higheft hopes!

COUNTESS.

You overrate,
With the warm impulfe of a noble mind,
My humble merits: but inform me, count,
—For in his abfence he muft be my theme—
Did never any difference arife,
—Such as, too oft' *has* ris'n 'twixt youth, and age—
Between my Albert, and his noble father?

COLMAR.

Nothing of moment:—nought, I truft, that left
Rankling rememb'rance.—Strict, himfelf, of morals,—
Tho' liberal, not profufe—perhaps he thought

His

His son's first burst of manhood rather wild,
And his expence beyond the bounds of prudence:
This, lady, I *have* heard, but this was *all*;
For never doating parent felt more pride
In a son's talents, and his manly grace,
Than felt the count in your accomplish'd lord's.

COUNTESS.

Thanks, noble sir, for gratifying thus
The fond enquiries of a curious woman;
Curious to ev'ry, ev'n the' least concern,
Of him she loves.—Marquis, *you* also know
My Albert's father?

MARQUIS.

Late, tho' long enough
To see, and feel his worth. Some six years since,
Upon a visit to a noble kinsman,
I often found admittance in this castle,
And learnt to love, and to revere its lord.

MATILDA.

But, my dear countess, you forget your purpose
To visit the fair terrace, whence the view
Of Alps on Alps, shining with all their snows,
O'er the dark forest of the tow'ring pines,
At once delights and elevates the soul.—

COUNTESS.

'Tis well remember'd; and the western sun
Must, at this moment, pour a golden blaze
On their white summits, and their lofty rocks.
Dear count, your arm.—Marquis, you'll shew the *way*,
And lead Matilda to her favorite seat.

D   [*Exeunt.*

SCENE II.

The great Hall, where enter BLAISE *and* TERESA.

TERESA.

You tell me wonders, I can hardly credit!
Can you believe the chambers you have mention'd
Are *really* haunted?—

BLAISE.

'Tis a ferious truth.—
Certain it *is*, that ere my prefent lord
Forbade accefs to thofe, and other rooms,
Certain it *is*, ftrange noifes oft' were heard
At dead of night: deep groans, and creaking doors;
And hurrying fteps, and hollow murmurings.—

TERESA.

O! let me never pafs within the view
Of thofe apartments!—I fhould die with fear
If I but heard the groans!—Hark!—What was that?
That ruftling found, along the vaulted roof?

BLAISE.

Nought but your fancy; or the rufhing wind
Againft the gothic cafements of the hall.

TERESA.

Are the apartments very far from hence?

BLAISE.

Quite at th' other extremity of the caftle:
The old count lov'd them for their privacy.

TERESA.

Thank Heav'n! or I fhou'd tremble at my fhadow.

But

But *now* the troubled fpirit is at reft?
No midnight noifes *now*?

BLAISE.

Yes, ftill, by night,
At times I've heard the found of paffing feet
And creaking hinges:—But the groans have long,
Long ceas'd.

TERESA.

The fpirit, then, has not *appear'd?*

BLAISE.

Never:—nor fince my mafter kept the keys
Of thofe apartments, have the groans been heard:
For when the rumour once had reach'd his ear,
Of midnight noifes and a walking ghoft,
He gave ftrict charge that no domeftic more,
Or paffing gueft, fhould fleep within *that wing*;
Then fhut it up, and keeps it from all notice.—

TERESA.

Think you my lord believes the rooms *are* haunted?

BLAISE.

I know not *that*; but *vaft* as is the manfion,
He never felt the want of thofe apartments,
And did not like report fhould circulate
The wond'rous ftory of his haunted caftle;
To frighten *fome*, to move the jeft of *others*,
And draw a curious gaping crowd around,
To watch for fpirits, and difturb his peace.
And who can blame him for the wife precaution?

TERESA.

What wou'd my noble lady give to fee
Thofe haunted rooms!—I've often heard her *talk*

Of

Of dreadful things, and fupernatural beings!
She thinks *fuch may* appear, but fears them not.
I never knew a lady of fuch courage!—

BLAISE.

Without the keys fhe cannot enter them,—
Nor has my mafter ever fhewn them fince.——
Nothing wou'd more offend him than to mention
So ftrange a tale,

TERESA.

Well, Blaife, another time
You'll tell me more; I now muft feek my lady.—

(*As fhe paffes by the table fees and takes up the
keys, left by the Count.*)

What keys are thefe?

BLAISE.

Three large ones, and a lefs!
I know the larger lead to thofe apartments
I told you of, The leffer one I know not:
The count, in hafte to go, has left them here,

TERESA.

I'm glad his caution has been *once* afleep;
I will convey them to my noble miftrefs,
And tell her all the marvels they fecure.—
Adieu! good Blaife.

BLAISE.

My dear Terefa ftay!—
Truft them to me!—It would difpleafe my lord
If any hint of what I've told were giv'n.
The countefs ought from *him* to hear the ftory,
When he fhall judge it proper to entruft her,

It

It is not fit for *us* to interfere
In such concerns as these!

TERESA.

Nay, nay, good friend,
If he has hitherto ne'er trusted *you*
To keep *these* keys, 'tis odds but he wou'd rather
My lady guarded them till his return.

BLAISE.

If not to *me*, entrust them to Lapont ;
The count in *him* has perfect confidence,

TERESA.

Think you *Lapont* is *trusted* like my *lady !*
To *her* the doating count has still reveal'd
His inmost thoughts,—He loves her with such paf-
fion,
And finds his tenderness fo *well return'd,*
That were his life and honor *both* at *stake,*
To *her,* with free and fearless confidence,
Wou'd *both* be trusted.—Rest *assur'd* of *this.*

BLAISE.

Enough: you ought to know their humours *best.*
But yet my heart misgives me that some trouble
Will surely spring from these forgotten keys.

TERESA.

Fear nothing ! I will fave you free from blame.

BLAISE.

I was to blame for tattling thus about them.
[*Exit one way, and Blaise the other, who paffes
Lapont hurrying back.*

Enter

Enter LAPONT *in great Agitation.*

LAPONT.

Where *are* thefe villanous keys? He left them *here*——
He *furely did!*—*accurfed* be my hafte
Not to fecure them, ere I followed him!
Perhaps old Blaife has found them.—If 'tis fo,.
I'll watch and found him well, but I will have 'em,
Yet ftill, Lapont, *beware* of *anxious* queftions.——
Such wou'd betray an earneftnefs about them,
Might lead to curious fearch, and *that* to *ruin*.
But yet fome prudent means *muft* be contriv'd
To get them back—'Tis of the laft importance
To *me*, the *count*, and to our mutual fafety!
This haughty beauty, overaws my foul.
I dare not face the ardors of her eye ;
It looks a fcorn I cannot brook, nor bear.
I dread her empire o'er her doating hufband ;
And if I cannot *fhake* it, foon will feize
Some lucky moment to fecure my fortune,
Then leave this caftle, and its hated owners.

[*Exit.*

Enter the MARQUIS, *and* MATILDA.

MARQUIS.

Repofe yourfelf! thefe fervent weftern rays
Have overpower'd you with oppreffive heat.

MATILDA.

Thanks to your kindnefs! I am much reliev'd,
And always moft delighted to receive,

—For

—For prudifh forms were idle with me now,—
Repeated proofs of your unvarying love.

" MARQUIS.

" Generous Matilda! Cou'd my paffion *cool*,
" This noble candor wou'd awake its warmth.

" MATILDA.

" Thus—with this pure, with this ingenuous ardor—
" *Thus* let us ever act, and ever love!"——
But I am pleas'd the countefs did not mark,
—Held in clofe converfe by her noble gueft,—
Our quick retreat.—" I know fhe's never weary
" Exploring fuch rare fcenes as nature here,
" Exulting, offers the enchanted eye:
" Sublime, as various; beautiful, as wild!"

MARQUIS.

She is a lovely, and a noble creature!
" I never faw fuch fpirit, and fuch foftnefs,
" So high a mind, with fo much courtefy;
" Such lofty manners, with fuch winning grace!"
I truft the count will merit the rare blefling
Which fortune has beftow'd, in fuch a wife.
How did he win her?—For fhe came upon us
Before you told me half I wifh'd to know
Of fuch a woman, and your chofen friend?

MATILDA.

In a few words; by ardent perfeverance,
His various talents, and his manly grace.
Yet, charming as he is, methinks the countefs
Eclipfes him, with her fuperior luftre.

MARQUIS.

MARQUIS.

Her rank and fortune, too, as I have heard,
Surpafs'd his own.—But abfent, long, from France,
And late return'd to peace and joy and love,
From all the dangers of the diftant war,
I know but little of events at home.

MATILDA.

Sole heirefs of the houfe of duke Pontac,
Her riches, birth, and wond'rous excellence,
Made her a match for many a fov'reign prince.
Such woo'd her; but magnanimous of foul,
" Unfway'd by intereft, or by vanity,"
She wou'd not marry, whom fhe cou'd not love.

MARQUIS.

Her houfe is of the nobleft France con boaft,
Which makes me wonder,—tho' the count himfelf
Bears a fair name, and owns an ample fortune,—
That her proud father wou'd confent her *hand*
Shou'd honour any, but of princely blood!—

MATILDA.

You know not how he doats upon his daughter!
When fhe affur'd him,—for her gen'rous foul,
Knows no difguife,—that to Montval alone
Her heart cou'd be prefented with her hand,
Tho' fomewhat loth, he gave his flow confent,
Sanction'd her paffion, and approv'd her choice,
And as *fhe* never knows a *lukewarm* feeling,
Never was man more ardently belov'd.—

MARQUIS.

Fortunate count! O! may his foul catch fire
At her bright flame, and emulate her virtue!

MATILDA.

MATILDA.

You feem to fpeak as fomewhat doubtful of him!
Have you heard aught that might *impeach his worth* !

MARQUIS.

I truft he is reform'd ; but well remember
When clofely link'd with the gay profligates
Which are at once, the fcourge, and fhame of Paris,
He plung'd, with *them,* in all the wild excefs,
And all the follies of that fplendid city.—

MATILDA.

I hope his riper years have feen the error.

MARQUIS.

I hope they *have* ; for graver manners mark'd
His public conduct, *ere* he *knew* the countefs,
And better maxims feem'd to take the lead
Of fenfelefs fquand'ring, and deftructive vice.

MATILDA.

I grieve to hear he *was* their votary ?
Ah ! never ! never ! may his noble bride
Know that his reputation fuffer'd blemifh
From vice, and follies, which her fpotlefs heart
Wou'd mourn *cou'd* taint the object of its love.

MARQUIS.

Be not difquieted ! for once renounc'd,
Vice fhews too hateful to allure us back,
And too repulfive, to feduce us more !—
But the day wanes.—The countefs foon will *join us* ;
Then let us enter, and await her prefence,—

[*Exeunt.*

E

Enter.

Enter Lapont, *and* Blaife.

LAPONT.

So honeft Blaife, you think your mafter's choice,
—That lofty countefs, with her lofty fcorn—
Does honour to his wifdom, and his tafte?

BLAISE.

Who *can* think otherwife, that fees her charms,
And knows my lady's virtue, wealth, and birth?

LAPONT.

Well, I confefs all *this :* but then her fpirit,
Her fpirit Blaife, may try thy mafter's temper!
She looks as if enamour'd of difdain,
And fhews a diftance to his old dependents,
—Moft *feelingly I fpeak!*—as if fhe fcorn'd
To *notice* any, but of *nobleft* blood,—
I wou'd not fuch a fpirit in wife!

BLAISE.

To *me* fhe fhews no fymptom of difdain ;
But is moft gentle, kind, and condefcending.

LAPONT.

That's mere caprice; for *thou* fhalt feel, ere long,
Her haughty temper, and imperious fcorn.
But now I think on't, haft thou found fome *keys*
The count, forgetful, left upon his table ?
He bade me feek them, as in friendly talk,
He held me to his coach.

BLAISE.

I have them not.

LAPONT.

LAPONT.

Nay! nay! this founds fo like equivocation!
Know you who *has*? or, did you fee them here?

BLAISE.

I need not tell you all I fee and know.—

LAPONT.

Granted my friend, But yet methinks this anfwer,
Night vex the count.—You know his hafty temper,
And know his value for the keys in queftion,
Which he has only trufted to *my care*.
It matters not to *me*.

BLAISE.

To fpeak the truth,
My lady's favou'rite woman found them here,
And faid fhe'd, ftraightway, give them to her *miftrefs*.

LAPONT *(agitated.)*

Give them the countefs!—run and ftop her Blaife!
But—yet—no matter *(afide)* " for fhe knows them not,
" Nor dreams of what importance"—'tis no matter.—
The keys are little worth; altho' the count,
For reafons thou haft heard, of ghofts, and groans,
And fuch ridiculous, and idle tales,
Chufes to have them in his *own poffeffion*.

BLAISE.

And fo I told Terefa.

LAPONT *(agitated.)*

So you *told* her!
Can nothing ever ftop thy bufy tongue!
How dare you *thus* reveal!—But never mind,
What care's thy mafter for the filly rumours.

E 2   Yet,

Yet, *wou'd* thou had'ft been *filent!*—Go and call
Young Ambrofe hither.—I've a meffage for him
Sent from the count, which I had near forgotten.

                        [*Exit.* Blaife.

I muft be quick! Deftruction feize them all!
            [*Takes pen, ink, and paper out*
                of his pocket, and writes.
So—So—'tis well—this, fure *muft* call him back
With eager hafte—

                (Ambrofe enters.)
        Come hither my good lad;
Clap on thy fpurs: faddle the fleeteft horfe
Thy mafter owns, and gallop after him
With thy beft fpeed.—It fhall be well rewarded!
Waking or fleeping fay thou com'ft from me,
And give this letter to his hand alone.—

               AMBROSE.
" Your pleafure fhall be done.   I know the road,
" And can o'ertake the Count ere one o'clock.

                  [*Exit Ambrofe.*

             LAPONT.
Ah! might he meet my wifh, he *now* were *here?*
I'll ftrive to watch the countefs, till he comes,
And counteract the mifery I dread,—
Cou'd I invent fome pretext might induce her
To *follow* her lov'd lord!—*Yes,*—that were *well.*
Curfe on his tendernefs!—had *I* been *by,*
Or had I once fufpected her *proud nature,*
I wou'd have interfer'd to *fpoil* their *marraige.*

                        But

But cou'd I meet Terefa ere *fhe* enters,
Much trouble and much terror might be fpar'd.
Curfe on thofe keys?---guarded with fo much *care*,
Recover'd once, they ne'er fhall fcape me more;
Or if they *fhox'd*, they fhall not then betray me.---

                            [*Exit.*

END OF THE SECOND ACT.

ACT III.

SCENE I—*The Great Hall. Enter the* COUNTESS
and the COUNT *of Colmars.*

COUNTESS.

Tempted by all the beauties of the scene,
Which caught new graces from the setting sun,
I thought not 'twas so *late.*

COUNT.

'Tis close of day.

COUNTESS.

So long shut up in all the smoke of Paris,
Loathing its noise, but more its hurrying life,
" Where ev'ry moment's *fill'd*, yet little done,
" By feeling hallow'd, or approv'd by reason ;"
These balmy breezes, whisp'ring health and peace,
And the soft calm that steals upon the soul,
Turning its thoughts to meditations high,
And converse sweet, made me forget the hour.
I hope the dews will not affect your health ?

COUNT.

By *choice*, accustom'd to a country life,
My nerves are strung to every change of season,
And brave, alike, the noon and midnight air.
You are too good to think of an old man
, With so much kindness !

COUN-

COUNTESS.

Ven'rable yourself,
Were you not Albert's father's chosen friend:
And can my heart be cold to such a claim?

COUNT.

Your approbation charms, and honours me.
But now 'tis time to thank your courtesy,
And take my leave.

COUNTESS.

What, at so late an hour!
We quarrel if to-night you quit the castle.

COUNT.

What shall I say? Commanding every heart,
Mine bends before you, and obeys your pow'r.
But, with your leave, I must difpatch my servant,
T'inform my wife and daughter of my purpose,
Left they expect and wait my *late* return.

COUNTESS.

At your good pleasure, sir.

[*Exit Count of Colmar.*
[*Countefs calls out* Ho! call Teresa!

Enter TERESA.

TERESA.

O! my dear lady! I have heard such things!

COUNTESS.

What things, Teresa?—What new fable now
Excites thy wonder, and awakes thy fear?

TERESA.

Look, madam, at these keys! Blaise says they
    open
The haunted rooms!

COUN-

COUNTESS.

You rave ! What haunted rooms ?

TERESA.

Where a wild fpirit walks, and groans by night ;
And rattles chains and locks, and fhakes the doors !

COUNTESS.

Doft thou not dream ? What idle tale is this ?
Give *me* the keys—How came they in your hands ?
And what unknown apartments do they open ?

TERESA.

The good old count's : he died in one of them.

COUNTESS.

And what of that ? Somewhere we all muft die.
Is *this* a reafon why the rooms are haunted ?

TERESA.

Indeed, my lady, it is *very true !*
Thefe dreadful noifes, and thefe groans *were* heard,
And ever fince the rooms have been lock'd up,
And the count keeps the keys himfelf.

COUNTESS.

The count !

TERESA.

Yes, madam : nor has any perfon fince,
Except himfelf, prefum'd to enter them.

COUNTESS.

Then by what means have you procur'd the
keys ?

TERESA.

As I was talking, madam, in the hall,
With good old Blaife, I found them on the table :
He told me what they open'd : and the count,
By fome ftrange chance, muft have forgotten them,

In

In hurry to depart ; for till that hour
Kept with the greateft caution—

COUNTESS *(interrupting her),*
You may go.
Let not this foolifh tale efcape your lips,
Nor proftitute my Montval's honour'd name,
By bringing it in proof of fuch romance !
Defire my friends wou'd fup, nor wait *my coming.*

[*Exit Terefa.*

I'm loft in wonder !—What can all this mean ?
But I will know if I have feen thefe rooms :
Perhaps I *have*, unconfcious of their fame.
No, no ! the caftle's vaft and intricate,
And if fome myft'ry hangs o'er thefe apartments,
The count had mention'd it while fhewing them.
Ha ! I remember now, before we parted,
He anxious feem'd that I fhould wait his prefence,
To wind th' entire lab'rinth of his caftle !—
I hate concealments !---They alarm and wound me,
From *him*, to whom, without *difguife*, my heart
Is always open, and fhou'd know, alike,
The fecret thoughts and foldings of his own !
Before the night is paft, I'll fee thefe chambers !
Thinking no ill, I fear none.—Innocence
Is the beft buckler, and the fureft guard
'Midft every danger, and for every fear.

(As fhe is going out, meets Lapont.)

A word, Lapont !—Say, did you fee my lord
After he left me to proceed to Paris ?

F

LAPONT.

LAPONT.

Yes, madam.

COUNTESS.

Did he send me any message?

LAPONT.

None, lady, but his love and deep regret
To be, so soon, divided from your arms.
But though he sent no message, he express'd
An earnest wish that you wou'd follow him,
As long this business might demand his absence.

COUNTESS.

Long might demand!—He said not so to me!

LAPONT.

Madam, if I may counsel—

COUNTESS (haughtily interrupting him).

You may counsel!
Pray know yourself, Lapont!—I always make
My equals, or my heart, my counsellors,
In the nice points of duty, or of love.
My noble guests may offer their advice;
But you presume in giving, till I ask it,

[Exit.

LAPONT.

School'd and contemn'd! confusion on her pride!—
Yet, high as she may think herself above me,
And far beyond my puny pow'r to touch her,
I yet may reach, and daunt her tow'ring soul!
I wou'd almost risk my life to humble her!—
Too well, before, I mark'd her scornful eye;
It seem'd to penetrate my inmost soul!—
But tho' her pride has cut me to the quick,

I joy

I joy to think she harbours no suspicion
About the keys, and their important trust.
All, then, is yet secure!--Cou'd I but meet
Her fav'rite woman, whose unguarded tongue
Tells all its knows, and whose unbounded fears
Dread ev'ry passing sound, much might be done!
But, to my wish, she comes!

Enter TERESA, *hastily.*

               Why, thus, in haste?
             TERESA.
My terrors brought me here?
             LAPONT.
                    What causes them?
Why sits pale fear upon thy lovely brow,
Like clouds that intercept the chearful day,
Obscuring all its charms?
             TERESA.
             You flatter, sir;
But I have cause, and cause enough for fear!
             LAPONT.
What cause, my fair one? Whisper it to me!
You know not, yet, your influence o'er my heart,
Which cannot taste content, while you are sad.
             TERESA.
O! you have, doubtless, heard the horrid tale,
Of midnight noises, and the haunted rooms?
             LAPONT.
What! has imprudent Blaise betray'd the secret
---For only he and I are privy to it---
The count has guarded with such jealous care?

                            That

That garrulous old fool muſt ſtill be talking,
And only death can ſtop his buſy tongue !
No doubt he told you ev'ry circumſtance !

TERESA.

He did ! he did ! And I ſhall die with fear,
If forc'd to wind the long dark galleries,
Without one friend to hear or comfort me !

LAPONT.

I'll be *that* friend, if you will take my counſel.
Beware you mention not this marv'llous ſtory
Among the ſervants ! 'Twou'd offend the count,
And loſe his favour !—But, *ſtill more* beware
Not to be prying for the troubled ſpirit !—
Once *I* but tried to open the apartment,
Daringly curious ! where it *nightly* walks,
Groaning, and clanking chains, and ſpouting fire,—
When ſuddenly my *hand* received a ſhock,
And then my *heart*, which long as life remains
I ſhall remember ! Heav'n forbid the hand
Which took ſome keys were left upon this table
Shou'd open with them the myſterious chambers !

TERESA.

Unhappy wretch ! O ! heav'n have mercy on me!
Why did I take thoſe unknown fatal keys,
And then deliver them to my dear lady ?

LAPONT (*aghaſt*).

What ! has the counteſs got the fatal keys ?

TERESA.

She *has* ! She *has* !—'Twas *I* who gave them her !

LAPONT (*eagerly*).

And did you talk to *her* about the ghoſt ?

TERESA.

TERESA.

O !—yes ! Alas ! I told her every thing !

LAPONT *(haftily).*

What did fhe fay ?

TERESA.

She treated it with fcorn ;
And if we can't perfuade her from her purpofe,
Her dauntlefs foul, which mocks my prudent fears,
Will furely tempt her to her own deftruction !

LAPONT.

Prevail with her to wait the count's return :
She knows his fondnefs can deny her nothing ;
And if fhe loves him, fhe will fhun his anger
By circulating, once again, the tale
His better judgment took fuch pains to filence :
But fhou'd your warning voice be difregarded,
Think you fhe'll dare to enter thofe apartments
Even by night ?

TERESA.

No, furely, *not* by *night*,
But in the morning fhe'll not fail to view them.
Pray you, good fir, attend me to the room
Where fit the ladies' women !

LAPONT.

I will guard you.
Make me your confident, whatever befalls,
And it may fave you from *fome dire misfortune !*

[*Goes out with her, but foon returns.*

This proud and daring woman fhakes my foul !
She curbs my power, and baffles all my art.
What *can* be done ? I dread her deep difcernment !

If

If fhe explores the chambers, I am loft !
Yet, fhe may *fearch*, and *fearch*, and not *difcover*!—
There lies fome *comfort!* Let her paufe to-night,
And I'll defy her prying fpirit after.
To-morrow's early dawn will bring the count,
And *then*, I earneftly will urge a meafure
Shall bid good-night, for ever, to our fears.
If he *deny me*, he muft ftand the trial,
But ftand alone ; for I'll abandon him
To all the fhame and peril of his fate.

[Exit.

SCENE—*Changes to the Saloon.*

Where appear the Count of COLMAR, *the* MARQUIS, *and*
MATILDA.

MATILDA.

I fear the countefs has fatigued herfelf,
Did you not mark her heavy alter'd eye ?

COUNT.

I *did*: but more there feem'd to me of thought,
Of careful thought, in her expreffive face,
Than wearinefs.——

MARQUIS.

I own, I think with *you*:——
A fomething furely preffes on her mind,
To caufe this fudden change.—When fhe return'd
Was fhe thus abfent, and abforbed in thought?

COUNT.

Quite the reverfe ! Her walk had giv'n her fpirits :
Enchanted with the glories of the fcene,
Her pure and animated heart expanded
At feeling, once again, the country's freedom,
And all the charms of renovated nature.

MARQUIS:

MARQUIS.

The dullnefs, and the lour of little minds,
Like the thin clouds that fleet before the breeze,
Affect me not : but when fuperior fouls
Turn inwards on themfelves, with fuch deep mufing,
The caufe is weighty, and I dread th' event.

COUNT.

Take it not thus! We all have ferious hours,
Which oft' depend on thoughts we can't command,
Born of thofe exquifite nerves, whofe finer tones
Difcordant thrill, we know not how or why.

MATILDA.

Yet mov'd without a caufe, I never knew her,
Free as fhe is from vapours or caprice,
And of a temper even, firm, and cheatful.
Profoundly touch'd fhe very rarely is ;
And never, but to fome important purpofe.

MARQUIS.

My dear Matilda, do not be alarm'd!
I truft your love, and not your judgment, conftrues
A ferious manner into ferious care.
" Remember too, that her dear lord is abfent ;
" For the firft time, divided from her arms !
" This, to a heart fo finely ftrung as her's,
" Is caufe enough to give her penfive moments.".

MATILDA.

Alas! I fear, there is fome other caufe.;
Tho' whence it cou'd arife I cannot guefs.

MARQUIS.

And is there need of other for her fadnefs ?
From the warm temper of your tender heart,
Which, form'd for pureft love, but light efteems

Its

Its own peculiar joys—with pride I fpeak—
When parted from the objeɛt of its choice ;
From your own heart, judge truly of your friend.

MATILDA.

" Your kind and generous nature, well I know,
" Would guard my timid foul from ev'ry care.
" But yet, remember, your own fears erewhile !

MARQUIS.

" Thofe fears were premature.—Be fatisfied !
" Nothing but Montval's abfence, reft affur'd,
" Has clouded over the fair countefs' brow."

MATILDA.

Pray heav'n it be fo !—But the count can tell us,
From his long intimacy in the caftle,
What is the charaɛter of this Lapont.
The countefs likes him not.——

COUNT.

         She fhews her judgment.
His foul a compound is of art and vice :——
Before his death, my friend difcarded him
For poifoning the morals of his fon,
By his bafe counfels.—Vile ingratitude !
For all the honors, and the favors done him !
And, I confefs, it touches me with wonder,
And, I may add, with grief, to fee the fon,
Th' accomplifh'd fon of fuch a matchlefs father
Carefs a villain who difgracees him !

MATILDA.

No wonder that my friend, fo pure herfelf,
Should feel repulfion at the wretch's prefence.
O ! if the count refpeɛts her as he ought,
He will abandon.—But the countefs comes.——

Enter the COUNTESS.

You'll pardon me, my friends, this little abfence.
To-morrow fhall atone for my omiffions.
With you I fhall be under no reftraint.
How wears the night ?

COUNT.

'Tis a late hour for fober folks like me.

COUNTESS.

After our walk, we all muft wifh to reft ;
And fweet the fleep that waits on exercife !
May it be your's, my friends, and fo good-night !
Bring in the lights !

[*Servants attend with lights.*]

          Attend my noble guefts
Unto their feveral chambers !—Nay ! no form !

MARQUIS.   MATILDA.   COUNT.

Fair be your dreams !—Adieu !—Lady, good night !
                         [*Exeunt.*

COUNTESS.

That's as it may be !—As the fpectre wills,
Which haunts my fancy in a thoufand fhapes,
And will not quit my troubled foul one inftant |—
" If I knew what to fear, it lefs wou'd move me :
Yet rather apprehenfion 'tis, than terror ;
A folemn feeling, than a weak difmay,—
Were not the name of him I love, involv'd
In this mifhapen tale, I fhould defpife it |
This makes me filent to my noble guefts.
Yet ! !—And I *blefs* the thought |—This goblin ftory
May have induc'd the Count,—and wifely too—

             G   To

To lock up the apartments ; left his peace,
And pride, fhould fuffer blemifh from the rumour,
Spread widely round, and turn'd, and magnified,
As ignorance, and fuperftition prompted !—
This fhall allay the tumult in my breaft,
And flatter downy flumber to my pillow !—
To-morrow then!—What ho! Terefe there !
Call up Terefa !—'Twas a bleffed thought !
I wou'd have done, juft as my lord has done !

Enter TERESA, *trembling.*

COUNTESS.

Why doft thou tremble ? Is it at thy fhadow ?—

TERESA.

O ! be not angry !—If you did but know !—

COUNTESS. (*angrily.*)

What !

TERESA.

What Lapont has told: what dreadful things !

COUNTESS.

Lapont ! ! !

TERESA.

O ! he has often heard the ghoft,
And fwears that trying to unlock the door,
It gave him fuch a fhock !—

COUNTESS. (*folemnly*)

I too am fhock'd !

TERESA.

Ah! for the love of Heaven reftore the keys,
Or the fierce fpirit will endanger you !
And fo Lapont believes.

COUNTESS. (*interrupting her*)

Only Lapont !—
Can thy hoarfe voice found nothing but Lapont !—
Go !—

Go !—Go to bed !—Thou and my other women !
I fhall not need your fervices to night.—
But not a word to them about the fpectre !
On my difpleafure, filence to them, and all !—
Yet, as you go, bid honeft Blaife come hither !—

                           [*Exit* TERESA.

My foul's on fire !—I will be fatisfied,
Betide what may !—Lapont is in the Plot !—
I've heard there are antipathies in nature,
And he is mine !—Why fhould my lord carefs him ?
And yet he does   Carefs, with confidence.
Nay, makes a favourite of the dangerous villain !—
But why a villain ?—'Tis his face alone,
The damning characters imprinted there,
That make me call him fo !—I hope, unjuftly !—

                Enter BLAISE.

Lady, your fervant humbly waits your orders !

               COUNTESS.

Blaife ! if your face belies you not, you're honeft ?
Honeft, I hope, and firm : fay, fhall I truft you ?

               BLAISE.

Lady, my hand, heart, life, are at your bidding !

               COUNTESS.

I'll never tempt thee to a dangerous fervice,
Nor to a deed that fhall difhonour thee !
Thou can'ft be fecret too ?   •

               BLAISE.

             Elfe were I bafe,
And little merited this condefcenfion.

               COUNTESS.

Be filent, or you forfeit my efteem !

               G 2   You

You know the rooms which idle rumour fays
Are haunted by a ghoft ?—What is their number ?

BLAISE.

An anti-room, a bed chamber, and clofet.

COUNTESS.

Direct me to them !—

BLAISE. (*aftonifhed*)
Madam !——

COUNTESS.
No reply !

I laugh at fpectres, and am bent to clear
Thefe ufeful chambers, of their ill report.

BLAISE. (*terrified*)
Lady ! indeed, my duty makes me fpeak.—

COUNTESS.
I've heard it all, and know 'tis fome impofture.
Be thou my guide ! for I will pafs this night,
Within the chamber where the fpirit walks !

BLAISE.
Now, Heav'n forbid !—

COUNTESS.
No more of foolifh fears !
Ev'ry attempt were vain to fhake my purpofe :
A chearful book and lights are all I need
To comfort, or defend me :—Thou fhalt watch
In th' anti-chamber by :—Now to my clofet,
And thence attend me to the haunted rooms.
[*Exeunt.*

END OF THE THIRD ACT.

ACT IV.

SCENE I.

The Antichamber to the Saloon.

Enter LAPONT *and* TERESA.

TERESA.

ALAS! I fear fhe's gone to that apartment!

LAPONT.

I wonder at fuch rafhnefs!—Are you fure
Your noble Lady is not in her chamber?

TERESA.

Wou'd that fhe were! She bade me call up Blaife,
And from that moment neither have been feen.

LAPONT.

It muft be fo!—Each circumftance confirms it:
She fent for him to fhew the haunted rooms,
But little knows the dangers fhe may run,
By braving the inexorable fpirit!
I know, by proof, its fierce vindictive nature.

TERESA.

O Heaven! Dear, kind Lapont, do not defert us!
How fhall we fave the too prefumptuous Countefs?
She may be loft if you cannot affift her.

LAPONT.

Be calm! To fave her life I'll rifk my own.
I yet

I yet, perhaps, may be in time to warn her.
From a bold enterprife may prove her ruin;
Caution and prudence, will do more than courage,
Where we encounter fupernatural things.—
Let the profoundeft filence feal your lips!—

TERESA.

O! doubt me not! In all you fhall direct.
But, pray! inform me of the Countefs' fafety:
My fears will almoft kill me till you come.

LAPONT.

Go to your chamber, where remain in peace
'Till I fhall feek you. Save your Lady's credit,
And doing fo, the honor of this houfe,
By keeping all a fecret from her guefts.—
This is of more importance than you think.
Truft all to me:—you fhall know more hereafter;
For my fond heart beats warmly in your favor.—
I'll fee you fafe, and then will feek the Countefs.
Truft to my friendly counfel, and fear nothing.

[Exeunt.

SCENE II.

*Changes to a fpacious Chamber, with a flately Bed, in
an Alcove. The Hangings of the Walls Tapeftry;—
a Couch, with a Table before it, on which is a Book
and Lights. The* COUNTESS *appears fpeaking to*
BLAISE, *who is pale, and trembling.*

COUNTESS.

'Tis well!—Nay,—why this tremor? Is there aught
To move thy fear?——

BLAISE.

BLAISE.

But, Lady! who can tell
How foon the ghoft!—'Tis after twelve o'clock!

COUNTESS.

Poor Blaife!—I fee how terror and obedience
Wage war within thy heart:—be not difmay'd!
I doubt I may have chos'n a ftouter guard:
However, Blaife, thy valor fhall not ftand
A trial too fevere. If I cry help,
Which will not be; affure thyfelf it will not—
Alarm the houfe; elfe watch without, in filence.

BLAISE, (as he goes out)

Thank Heav'n I am difmifs'd!—Wou'd morn
were come! [Exit BLAISE.

COUNTESS.

And now to fcrutinize this marvellous chamber.
It is a noble one; and might be turn'd
To better purpofe, than to harbour ghofts!—
The tapeftry is rich, and little worn:
The bed is fumptuous;—every thing complete,
And all in order:—
I can find nothing, yet, to caufe alarm;
And, doubtlefs, all has fprung from fuperftition,
The child of ignorance, and flavifh fear!
But why this fmaller key fufpended hence?
The flighteft trace of any other door
Cannot be found: except the dreffing-room;—
That's open; and this key fits not the lock.—
But what it leads to, is not worth conjecture.—
I'll to my book; and fleeping, for this night,
Upon that couch, perhaps may dream of ghofts,

2   Which,

Which, waking, I have neither heard, or feen.

> [*Takes up the book, but prefently reclines
> on the couch, and begins to dofe.*]

SCENE III.

Changes to the Anti-Chamber, where BLAISE *is feen
gently opening the Door a little which leads to the
inner Apartment.*

BLAISE.

Thank Heav'n! all's quiet, and my lady fleeps!
I truft the horrid fpectre is at peace,
And ne'er will come to trouble us again!
O! that a woman fhould poffefs fuch courage!

LAPONT.

> [*Gently opens the outward door, faying
> foftly*]

Hift! hift! Blaife! hift!

BLAISE.

Mercy! what noife was *that!*

LAPONT.

It is a friend! Lapont! be not afraid!
I come to guard, and not to injure thee!—

BLAISE.

Now, Heav'n be prais'd! I fear'd it was the ghoft!
Enter, good Sir! O! welcome, kind Lapont!
I am exceeding glad to fee you here!

LAPONT.

I know thou art.   But where's thy noble lady?

BLAISE.

Hufh! hufh!—She's faft afleep in yonder chamber.

LAPONT.

LAPONT. *(Pleafed and eagerly)*
Afleep d'ye fay !—Are you quite fure fhe fleeps ?
·BLAISE.
Come gently this way, and yourfelf may fee her.
Look thio' the door.

LAPONT.
Thank Heav'n ! fhe is afleep !
Sound be her flumbers !—Then we, ftill are fafe !
How long is't fince fhe enter'd.thefe apartments?

BLAISE.
Scarcely, I think, an hour has paft away..
Ere I fet all in order, and came hither.

LAPONT.
Did fhe difcover no furprife, or terror,
On·looking round the gloomy haunted room?

BLAISE.
No! not the leaft.

LAPONT.
Nor have you heard her fince,
Exclaiming loud ? nor have the found of locks,
Or hollow groans, or creaking hinges fcar'd you ?

BLAISE,
Nothing! O! Heaven! I tremble at the thought!

LAPONT.
Why art thou here ? Was it by her command
Thou thus art plac'd her patient centinel ?

BLAISE.
It was : and ftrictly that command enjoin'd
That I fhou'd watch, in filence, till I heard
Her voice demanding help.

LAPONT.
I'm fatisfied.

H   BLAISE.

BLAISE.

But who, Lapont, inform'd you I was here?

LAPONT.

Teresa stealing to her lady's chamber
And finding she was absent, in a fright
Ran straight to me: I quickly guess'd the plot,
And came to warn, or help, as things requir'd.
But since she is asleep, I trust the ghost
Will not appear to harm, or trouble her.—
'Tis past the time when it is wont to walk.

BLAISE.

But if it shou'd!!

LAPONT.

Be you upon the watch,
And see, from time, to time, the Countess sleeps!
Her safety may depend upon this caution.—
If any noise is heard; as groans, or talking,
Or creaking doors, or sound of opening locks,
Run, quick, to me,—I'll watch in my own room—
And give alarm!—Be wakeful on thy life!—

[*Exit.*

BLAISE. (*As he goes out.*)

O! trust me, good Lapont! I will not fail.

[*Shuts the door cautiously, of the inner
Chamber, then takes a cordial bottle
from his pocket and drinks.*]

My mind is more at ease: This shall support me.
'Tis half past one, and my old eyes are heavy:
There is no danger from the ghost to night!
So I may safely venture, like my lady,
To court the comfort of refreshing sleep.—

[*Pushes an arm chair behind the side scene
to repose in, and Exit.*]

SCENE

SCENE IV.

Changes to the Inner Chamber, where, while the COUN-
TESS *still doses ; a long and deep Groan is heard, she
starts, and half rising, exclaims.*

COUNTESS.

Did I not hear some noise?—Or was't the wind?
  *[Another deep groan ; on which she starts
   up, greatly agitated.]*
What dismal found was that ?—Whence cou'd it
come !
   [Repeated groans.]
Again !—again !—It came from that alcove !
Be not appall'd, my soul !—Thou'st done no wrong !
  *[As she advances, with great emotion to-
   wards the alcove, another groan is more
   distinctly heard.]*
Almighty God ! if 'tis some troubled spirit .
Permitted, by thy will, to walk by night ;
Give me the grace to send it to the grave,
Whate'er his cause of misery, in peace!
   [More groans ; she starts aghast.]
O !—speak !—appear !—reveal the secret trouble
That forceth thee to leave the silent tomb,
And roam 'midst darkness, and the midnight airs!
   [Groans repeated.]
Now Heav'n sustain me, and enlighten me,
To fathom this dread secret !—Hence ! e'en hence
The moaning issued, as if under ground !
  *[She looks with wild horror round the
   alcove.]*
   H 2   Yet,

Yet, more diftinct, as from fome hollow cavern!
Hah!—From the tapeftry!—My foul's wound up
To utmoft agony of dread fufpenfe,
And I fhall madden if——

> [*Lifts up a loofe part of the tapeftry, and
> difcovers a door.*]

                    What's here!—A door!
A fecret door! And this the fateful key

> [*Haftily fnatching the keys; unlocking the
> door.*]

That leads to what, at once, I wifh, and fear!—

> [*Groans very diftinct.*]

Nay, then, there is no paufe!—Narrow, and dark,
And fteep, as is the way, and chill the air,
Something impels me on, and I muft go!
Be God my great protector, and my guide!—

> [*She difappears, but foon rufhes back with
> looks of amazement and horror.*]

Eternal pow'rs!—I faw it thro' the gloom!
Tho' indiftinct!—I heard its hollow groans!—
They pierc'd my heart, and curdled up my blood!—
Bafe fears! Why have ye thus fubdued my foul!
If it fhou'd follow, I will fpeak to it.—
Hark!—It approaches!—O! ye pow'rs above!
Equal my courage to the dread occafion!—

> [*The tapeftry is lifted up flowly, and dif-
> covers the pale, and haggard, yet reve-
> rend figure of an Old Man, with a long
> white beard, and difordered hair, and
> dreffed in a long flowing black robe, who
> fpeaks, as he enters.*]

                                        OLD

OLD MAN.

This way it beckon'd me, and I will follow.

[*Seeing the Countefs, he is awe-ftruck, and exclaims.*]

What heavenly vifion's this !—Angel of light !
Say ! Art thou come,—fo long, fo often call'd !—
To end my mifery, and bear my fpirit,
Where it, at laft, may reft ?—

COUNTESS. *(Approaching)*

Art thou the ghoft ?

OLD MAN.

I am, indeed, the fhadow of myfelf,
My former felf !—But what art thou, bright vifion ?

COUNTESS.

A weak, and erring creature, like thyfelf.—

OLD MAN.

If not an angel, as 1 fondly hop'd !
Come to releafe me from my fecret dungeon ;
Where lingering years of agonizing grief,
And racking pain, without one ray of comfort,
Have bow'd me down in hopelefs mifery !—
Why art thou here ? And wherefore didft thou come
To fhoot one cheering glance athwart my gloom,
Then quick withdraw the beam ?—

COUNTESS.

Years, didft thou fay !
Years haft thou languifh'd in that dreary place,
The very glimpfe of which appall'd my foul ?

OLD MAN.

Alas ! 'tis very long, or fo it feems,
To one who only knows to count the hours
By the chill damps that drop upon his head,

Or

Or by his fighs, and tears!—'Tis very long!
Since I was torn from the dear light of day,
Reft of all comfort, and cut off from man!

COUNTESS.

I'm almoft breathlefs with aftonifhment, and pity,
And fcarce can afk if Montval!—if my hufband!—
If by his rigour, thou fo long haft fuffer'd?·

OLD MAN. *(afide)*

" O! 'tis his wife! Refign'd,—fo near my end,
" I won't accufe him!—They may live in peace!"

COUNTESS.

Why doft thou turn, and mutter to thyfelf?
Speak out thy griefs, and tell me for what crime—,

OLD MAN *(interrupting her)*

Be Heav'n my judge that none have brought me
here!

COUNTESS.

Then who?—what tyrant, rough and pitylefs!
Immur'd thee thus, to die a living death?

OLD MAN.

Know you Lapont?—That villain was the caufe!

COUNTESS *(exultingly)*.

I faid he was a villain!—O! a load,
A heavy load is taken from my heart!—
Whate'er thy guilt, I wou'd not that Montval,
My dear Montval! had been fo bafe of foul,
To take fuch vengeance on thy helplefs age,
For worlds, on worlds!—But, he muft know thy
    fate!——

OLD MAN.

Plac'd on the brink of dread eternity,
I dare not lie!—He does;—but is mifled
By the vile mifcreant whom you juftly hate.

COUNTESS

COUNTESS.

Mifled!—O bitter!—Can he fee thy dungeon,
And look upon thy anguifh, and thy age,
And not relent!—It cuts me to the foul!—
But tell me what, and whence, and who thou art?

OLD MAN.

Afk not what never fhall efcape my lips,
For potent reafons:—nought can wreft it from me!

COUNTESS.

" Amazing!—But thou fhalt no longer fuffer!
" I will releafe thee, of my own free will;
" And thou fhalt live, and be reftor'd to comfort!
" Thy miferies well may expiate thy guilt!—
" And for Lapont! if he has injur'd thee,
" That hateful villain! he fhall have his meed!
" Be fure he fhall!"——

OLD MAN.

Dim is my fpark of life!
Yet, to the laft, we cherifh liberty!
But all revenge is dead within my heart,
And ill I fhou'd repay your generous pity,
By fowing difcord 'twixt your lord and you.

COUNTESS.

O! foul of noblenefs and charity!
Rever'd old man! Tax me to th' very utmoft!
And I can much!—Tax all my pow'r and fortune!
For guilt ne'er harbour'd in a heart like thine.

OLD MAN.

Thou noble creature!—I am too weak to bear
This rufh of gratitude, fo long weigh'd down
By wrong, and cruelty, and pain, and forrow!

COUNTESS.

COUNTESS.

Be not dejected!—Hide not, thus, your face!

OLD MAN.

A thousand tender, painful recollections
Press down, and almost suffocate my heart!

COUNTESS.

What can this mean!—What dreadful mystery!

OLD MAN.

O! may it still a mystery be to you!——

COUNTESS.

'Tis wonderful! But go with me from hence!
" I hate to be so near that horrid dungeon!"

OLD MAN.

I will, on this condition.—That your lord
Shall never see me more. That you ne'er ask
Of him, or others, who, or what I am;
And that I part unseen by all but you!

COUNTESS.

Astonishing!—But only go with me,
And have thy wish.—My lord is gone to Paris.
Why then delay?

OLD MAN.

Allow me yet some pause!
What is the hour? For, buried from the light,
Darkness and day have been alike to me!

COUNTESS,

'Tis scarce above two hours from now to morn.

OLD MAN.

How learn'd you I was here? Or how depart,
At such an undue hour, without alarm?

COUNTESS.

How I discover'd you, at full, hereafter,

I   You

You fhall be told :—to leave this night the Caftle,
Without fufpicion, were not poffible.
But if refolv'd to go without delay,
To-morrow's dawn fhall find the ready means
To fend you hence, unknown to all but me.

OLD MAN.

" Have you the keys ?

COUNTESS.

" I have.

OLD MAN.

" But how procur'd ?

COUNTESS.

" By a mere chance, it were too long to tell.
            [*Recollects* BLAISE, *and looks into the an-
            ti-room.*]
" Hah ! I had forgot !—'Tis well, he's faft afleep.

OLD MAN. *(alarmed)*

" Who's in that chamber ?

COUNTESS.

" Only Blaife, the fteward ;
" Set there by me, to watch, and give alarm,
" If aught requir'd.——

OLD MAN.

" But has he overheard us ?

COUNTESS.

" O'erfpent with watching, he profoundly fleeps.

OLD MAN.

Then, by my fufferings, and my innocence !
By that benevolence, which born of heaven,
Lives in your gen'rous heart, and from your eye

I   Beams

Beams melting pity on a ſtranger's woe,
Back to my dungeon let me go, once more,
And paſs the interval from now, till morn!—
O! grant me this requeſt!—

COUNTESS.
　　　Not for the world!
My pow'r, if needful, ſhall protect you here
From every wrong.

OLD MAN.
　　　Dear lady! be advis'd!
Lapont muſt miſs the keys, and will be waking;
For guilt, like his, is ever on the watch:
Too well I know my cruel, crafty goaler!
" And now, when all your bidding might com-
　　mand,
" Are, thro' the caſtle, ſunk in deep repoſe,
" It were not ſafe to truſt a villain's vengeance.
" So great his malice, and ſo black his crimes,
" That even your rank, and pow'r might fail to
　　ſave you:
" I wou'd not, for the world, he ſaw us here!
" 'Twou'd, ſurely urge him to ſome deſperate
　　deed!
" Nor ſhall my name, or perſon be reveal'd
" To your domeſtics: This my firm reſolve,
" The hope of liberty ſhall never alter!"

COUNTESS (Aſide.)
" Blaiſe muſt know nothing. It were better thus:"
I'm loth to leave you in that diſmal place.

OLD MAN.
　　The brightneſs of your angel countenance,
Still preſent to my ſoul, ſhall give me light,

　　　　　　　　　　　　　　　　And

And fpread effulgence thro' furrounding gloom!
At morn I will attend you.

COUNTESS.

" Be it fo,
" Since fo you will. But I fliall count the hours,
" Till fweet deliverance greets you by my hand.
[*Afide.*] " Myfelf will watch and guard him till the
    dawn."

OLD MAN.

" Think you a few fhort hours which furely lead
" To light, and liberty, and long-loft friends,
" Think you they can feem long, to me feem long,
" Who years on years have languifhed in a dungeon?

COUNTESS.

" At leaft thefe conferves, and this added light,"
May help to cheer you, till we meet again!
I will myfelf, conduct you to your prifon.
Nay, no reply. I will not be refus'd.

[*Exeunt, fhe fupporting him.*]

SCENE V.

Changes to LAPONT's *Room where he appears walking*
about, much agitated.

LAPONT.

I cannot reft! guilt, terror, and revenge,
With mingled violence, wake a hell within me!
If I fhou'd fall, I will not fall alone.
The Countefs, and her virtues I abhor!

I 2   Her

Her very beauty, to my eye, is hateful!
It fafcinates, and overawes the Count,
And blafts my fortune, when the fruit grew ripe.
I was a fool not to make all things fure
Before this haughty meddling woman came!
Oh! fhe fhall learn how dangerous 'tis to goad
A refolute heart, that glories in it's guilt,
When independence, pow'r, or pleafure tempt!
That prating Blaife!—I muft be rid of him.
Terefa I can fool to all I wifh.
But while my bofom broods its embryo purpofe,
Silent and dark. The Count will hurry back!
That muft be thought of. I am fafe to-night,
And for to-morrow's fafety, and to-morrow's,
Long as the term of my ftrong life fhall laft,
My courage, and my cunning fhall provide.

Enter BLAISE *haftily, pale, and trembling.*

BLAISE.

Lapont! Lapont! the Countefs!

LAPONT (*Agitated*)
What of her?

BLAISE.

Is murder'd by the ghoft, or borne away!

LAPONT.

You rave, or dream! How borne away! how
murder'd!

BLAISE.

Alas! I know not! But fhe is not there!

LAPONT

LAPONT (*Eagerly*)
Not where?

BLAISE.
Not in the chamber where you left her.

LAPONT.
How cou'd fhe go without your hearing her?

BLAISE.
Heavy with watching, fleep, at laft furpris'd
me.

LAPONT (*Furioufly*)
Thou hoary wretch. [*Afide.*] " But I muft curb
my rage."
" She has found the fecret door, and I am loft!
" Hah! That's the only way!

BLAISE.
What can be done?

LAPONT (*Afide*)
" There is no time for hefitation now,
" Forc'd to a point, peril on either fide,
" One way, and only one can lead to fafety."
Come this way Blaife, into my clofet here!
I have fomething there to fay of great importance.

[BLAISE *enters with him, but is prefently
heard crying out.*]
O! do not murder me! for mercy's fake!

LAPONT (*Behind the Scene*)
Dotard! take that! Go, fleep, for ever now!
[*He then enters with bloody hands, and a
dagger.*]
So! one is fafe. That fool can blab no more!

This

This key will make me master of his hoard :—
A comfortable sum, in time of need !
Happen what may, I shall not fear Montval,
And may enjoy my bloody spoils in peace,
Without the dread of his pursuing vengeance.
Nay, such is my ascendance o'er his mind,—
That all I execute, he shall approve,
And largely pay me for my secrecy.
'Tis almost dawn.   I will but cleanse my hands,
And ease that miser's coffer of its gold,
And then my dagger flies at nobler prey.

                         [*Exit.*

END OF THE FOURTH ACT.

ACT V.

SCENE I.

A Gallery.

Enter MATILDA *and* MARIA, *in great conſternation.*

MATILDA.

NOT in her chamber? nor has been to night?
　　What wonders have I heard? Am I awake?
Can it be true, the ſtory thou haſt told,　.
Of haunted rooms, and of a nightly ſpectre?

MARIA.

'Tis but too true.　And having told the tale
To my dear lady, who has got the keys,
I thought it right to rouſe you from your reſt,
And mention all I knew.

MATILDA.

　　　　　Thou haſt done well
To break my ſleep, where ſhe may be in danger.
Yet what the danger, Heav'n alone can tell,
From ſuch a ſtrange, and ſenſe-confounding cauſe!
Wou'd thou hadſt been diſcreet, and held thy tongue,
About theſe wonders, till the Count's return.

2　　　　　　　　　　　　　　MARIA.

MARIA.

Ah! wou'd I had been filent! But my fears
Betray'd my prudence; thoughtlefs of th' event.

MATILDA.

Where lie the chambers which 'tis faid are haunted?

MARIA.

Alas! I know not! Blaife, if he were here,
Cou'd fhew the way; and fo cou'd good Lapont,
Who, urg'd alike by courage and by zeal,
Hurried to feek, and to protect the Countefs.

MATILDA.

A dreadful apprehenfion feizes me!
I like not fuch protectors! Deareft friend!
The fearlefs temper of thy gen'rous mind
May urge thee on to unfufpected peril!
My heart is on the rack till thou art found.
Thou cou'dft not bear Lapont! And thy fure eye
Has never fail'd to read a villain's heart.
What can be done? Knock at the Marquis' door?
Call up the Count?—The Count?—Ha! he can
guide,
Can furely guide us to thofe horrid chambers.
That way he fleeps. Be quick, and give alarm!

[*Exit* MARIA.

Why wou'd the Countefs run this needlefs hazard?

[*Exit.*

[LAPONT *enters cautioufly from the other fide.*]

LAPONT.

Now is the time, when all are wrapt in fleep!
All but my victims, who fhall feel my arm!
Since every project to prevent this woman,

This

This haughty woman, from her fatal prying,
Has been the means, by fome accurfed chance!
Of urging her to fathom the dread fecret.
But fhe as well might have effay'd to crufh
The deadly ferpent with her delicate hands,
As to deftroy, or counteraĉt my vengeance!
Now her proud fpirit——

> [*Count of* MONTVAL *enters from the other*
> *fide of the ftage, with an air of diftrefs*
> *and difmay.*]

" He return'd fo foon!
" Too early, yet too late!"

COUNT.

What now Lapont?
Is aught difcover'd? Hell itfelf is here!
[*Striking his bofom.*]
And thou the demon that has made it fo!—
O! had I never liften'd to thy counfel!

LAPONT.

'Twere wafte of time or I cou'd anfwer you.
Keep your own fecret, and you've nought to fear!

COUNT.

Yes! Confcience! Confcience! waking, but too
late!
I loath myfelf, my crime, and its fuccefs!
Nor time, nor circumftance can ever cure
The living ulcer, that corrodes my heart!
Forc'd to adore, by that unerring juftice,
Which all our arts can neither bribe nor blind,—
The radiant virtue which my deeds pollute,

K   My

My foul can never tafte of comfort more !
O ! never! never!——

LAPONT.

Wretched canting this !
Worthy the bigot monk, and cloifter'd cell,
Where folitude and fafting ape the tone
Of coward penitence, and pious zeal !

COUNT.

In vain ! you mock the horrors I endure !
They merit fympathy, and not derifion,
And moft from thee, the partner of my guilt.
How can I face the Countefs !—how fupport
Her pure embraces !

LAPONT (*fneeringly*). ..

Trial too fevere !—
But, if you value her efteem, or love,
For fhou'd fhe know you, both were loft for ever,
Quickly depart !—Away! with fpeed, for Paris,
And never let her know of your return.

[*Afide.*]

" His confcientious qualms muft not be trufted."

COUNT.

But are you certain fhe has no fufpicion ?

LAPONT.

Back! back! where welcome tidings fhall await
    you.
I'll foon be mafter of the fatal keys :
The Countefs tried, and laugh'd at all they fhew'd
    her.
The fecret door, to her's a fecret ftill.
Away! away ! or we may be difcover'd !

Terefa

Terefa has the keys, and they'll be mine.

[*Afide, going out.*]

" Poor eafy dupe! he credits all I fay !"

COUNT.

Determin'd villain! had I never known thee,
I had been bleft ! But I muft ftill diffemble,
Till the time's riper to defy his malice.
I'll go and order that my horfe be ready,
Juft look, tho' loth, towards the hated chamber,
To fee that all is ftill, and all fecure,
And then, with heavy heart! depart for Paris.

[*Exit.*

SCENE II.

Changes to the fuppofed Haunted Chamber. The
COUNTESS *rifes from the Couch and comes forward.*

COUNTESS.

The fun is rifing. I will fpeak to Blaife,
Difmifs him to procure a clofe conveyance,
Ignorant for whom, or what it is defign'd—
And then releafe the patient fufferer.
His look and manners move my inmoft foul!
What deep affront; what motive for revenge,
Cou'd make the Count abet fuch cruelty!
There is a fecret in this ftrange affair
I cannot fathom ! The afflicted victim
With Chriftian meeknefs, fhudders to accufe
My guilty Lord, in fpite of all he has fuffer'd!

K 2   O!

O! Montval! Montval! clear this myftery
And clear thyfelf, or never can my heart
Efteem thee. more!

> [*Goes to the Door leading to the Anti-*
> *Chamber and calls out.*]

> What Blaife! Awake!

> Ha! gone!

Then it is time, indeed, to feek the captive,
And to conceal him in mine own apartment,
'Till private means are fought for his departure.

> [*Enters the Door leading to the Dungeon,*
> *and difappears.*]

SCENE III.

Changes to the Dungeon.

PRISONER,

It can't be far from morn! This precious light,
Precious! becaufe her angel hand beftow'd it.
Is nigh extinct!—I thought I could have borne
This fhort delay, with a more equal mind!
Oh! that I might but prefs her to my heart,
And call her!—But my guardian fpirit comes!

COUNTESS.

Thou venerable man, whoe'er thou art;
I come to lead thee to the chearful day!
But time is fhort, and circumftances prefs!

PRISONER.

My tutelary angel! I obey!——

> [*As he is going out with her, enter* LAPONT
> *with a Dagger in his Hand.*]

> That

That villain here! Then heav'n indeed defend
us!

LAPONT.

Aye! fay your prayers, for you have need of
them!

COUNTESS *(Advancing)*

Infolent wretch! What means this bold in-
trufion?

How dare you fet yourfelf to watch my fteps!
Villain avaunt! and never face me more!—

LAPONT *(Awe ftruck a moment, Afide)*

"What fhall I faulter at a woman's frown!"
Perhaps, indeed, we ne'er may meet again!

COUNTESS.

Obdurate monfter! I can guefs thy purpofe!
That dagger and thy face are well agreed!
The midnight murderer, is mark'd by both!

[*As he advances towards her, fhe fteps
back, and draws a Dagger from her
Bofom.*]

Affaffin, look!—I have a dagger too?
But to defend, not murder innocence!
Advance one ftep, and I will ftrike thee dead!

LAPONT *(Afide)*

"My fate is fix'd, there's no retracting now!"
Imperious woman! thus I anfwer thee!

[*He rufhes on her, and attempting to feize
the Dagger with which fhe attempts to
ftrike him; in the ftruggle it falls.*]

COUNTESS.

Audacious ruffian!

LAPONT.

LAPONT.

This to prove me fo.

[*As he feizes her by the Arm, and is about
to plunge his Dagger in her Bofom, the
old Prifoner takes up that which had
fallen, and plunges it in his Side.* LA-
PONT *falls.*]

PRISONER.

Thus righteous heav'n affifts the feeble arm!

LAPONT.

Oh! damn'd furprife! may hell and furies feize
thee!
Vengeance and horror! But I will not die!
I am not prepar'd.

[*Trying to rife, falls and expires.*]

PRISONER.

Alas! thou art not prepared,
To meet the juftice of offended Heav'n!

COUNTESS.

Quick, let us haften from this dreadful dungeon.

PRISONER.

My feeble limbs, exhaufted by this effort,
Refufe their office!—I muft reft awhile!

COUNTESS.

Nay, lean on me! I pray you lean on me!
I will fupport you! and in juftice ought,
Since but for you, I were a lifelefs corfe!

Exeunt flowly, fhe fupporting him.

SCENE

SCENE IV.

The fuppofed haunted Room, where appear the COUNT *of* COLMAR, *the* MARQUIS, MATILDA, *and* MARIA, *in great conflernation.*

MATILDA.

She is not here! I fhall grow mad with terror!

MARQUIS.

Be calm my love!—Yet, yet fhe will be found!
Think not this fabled phantom can endanger
Your noble friend.

COLMAR.

There's fomething more in this
Than a mere fhadow. Heard you not fome noife?

MATILDA.

Towards th' alcove?

MARQUIS.

It was.—Again I hear it!

MATILDA.

O! I fhall faint!—Now! now! I hear the murmur
Of fome fad voice!

COUNT.

The found of feet approaches,
Yet nothing's feen!—Nearer! yet nearer ftill!

MATILDA.

Protect me Marquis! See!—the tapeftry!

> [*The tapeftry is lifted up, and difcovers
> the* COUNTESS *fupporting the* OLD
> COUNT, *whofe face is ftained with
> blood.*]

MARQUIS.

MARQUIS.

Eternal Pow'r! what apparition's this!

TERESA.

O! Heav'n defend us!

MATILDA.

I fhall die with terror!

[*As the* OLD COUNT *advances towards
an eaft window, he averts his face, exclaiming.*]

The light! the light!——

[*And faints.*]

COUNTESS.

O God! the victim dies!

[*All gather round.*]

MARQUIS.

Fly, fly for fuccour!   [*Exit* MARIA.

COUNT OF COLMAR.

Can the grave reftore!!

My eyes deceive me!—No!—it is my friend!—
But, ah! how chang'd!

COUNTESS. (*with great emotion*)

What can you mean?—What friend?

COLMAR.

The Count of Montval! Nobleft, beft of men!

[YOUNG COUNT *enters, who, feeing his
father, ftands horror-ftruck.*]

COUNTESS.

Of Montval?—What!—the father!——

YOUNG COUNT.

Swallow me, earth!—

COLMAR.

COLMAR.

O! yes, the father of thy noble hufband!

. COUNTESS.

Accurs'd the found! and blotted be the hour,
That fhews a monfter—in the man I lóv'd!

MARQUIS.

What dreadful mifery! what horrid crime
Has buried thus alive!—

COLMAR.

The Count revives!

[OLD COUNT *raifes himfelf a little, fup-
ported by the* COUNTESS *and* COLMAR.]

OLD COUNT.

O! I am fick!—fick unto death!—So!—fo!—
Here let me lean!

[*Reclining his head on the* COUNTESS'
bofom.]

COUNTESS.

O! live!—But try to live,
Or the moft abject wretch that crawls on earth,
Is bleft, compar'd with me!

OLD COUNT.

What haft thou faid,
Nobleft and kindeft!——Ha!—my cruel fon!

[YOUNG COUNT *throws himfelf at his
father's feet, the* COUNTESS *averting
her face from him with ftern horror.*]

YOUNG COUNT.

Yes! from my bofom rend this barbarous
heart!
Trample my body!—Curfe my impious foul!—
All is too good for fuch a fon as me!

L OLD

OLD COUNT.

Do'ft thou repent?

YOUNG COUNT.

Repentance is too calm!
Remorfe and horror tear my burfting heart!

OLD COUNT.

Then may thy God forgive, as I forgive thee!

YOUNG COUNT.

Enchanting found!·But live! O! live to blefs
me!

[*Enter* TERESA.]

OLD COUNT.

It will not be!—I fear—it will not be!

COUNTESS (*fuddenly turning, and taking the cordial from* TERESA.)

O! fwallow this!—It may revive your fpirits!
Think of my agonies!—My dread defpair!

OLD COUNT. (*trying to drink*)

I cannot fwallow!—my emotions choak me!—
This fudden change! this conflict—is too much
For age and weaknefs—worn with length of forrow!

COUNTESS. (*fternly to her bufband*)

Canft thou hear this, and not be turn'd to ftone!

OLD COUNT. (*to her*)

Be comforted!—Forgive, as I forgive him!
[*To his fon.*]
Cherifh the beft and nobleft of her fex,
And thus redeem thy injuries to me!
Quick, let me feal thy pardon ere I die!—
[*Embraces him feebly.*]
My good and dear old friend, your hand once more!
[*Giving his hand to* COLMAR.]

Daughter,

Daughter, may ev'ry blessing———
      [*Sinks and dies.*]

     COUNTESS. (*starting up wildly*)
         Blessing!—!!—
Can I be blest! link'd to a parricide!—
See!—see! his hands reek with a father's gore!
O! murder!—murder!—Has thy iron heart
No touch of nature!
    [*Stands as if gasping for breath.*]

      MATILDA.
   Dearest, dearest friend!
Now let your wonted firmness stand the test,
And calm your anguish!

      MARQUIS.
     'Tis a dreadful trial
For love and virtue, such as her's, to bear!

     YOUNG COUNT.
  Well may she loath a guilty wretch like me!
I dare not ev'n approach!—Yet, if my love!—
If deep remorse———

    COUNTESS. (*starting from her stupor*)
     Thy love!—detested love!—
What can remorse, where crimes have dy'd, the
    soul
So deep a black!—Go!—herd with cannibals,
Who feed on human flesh, and drink man's blood!—
Yet, even they, respect and love their fathers!—

     YOUNG COUNT.
  Soul-harrowing thought!—Yet, gracious Heav'n
   can pardon
The guiltiest wretch that lives beneath the skies!

      L 2   COUNTESS.

COUNTESS.

O mifery! madnefs!—All my brain's on fire!—

MATILDA.

Let reafon fpeak to check thefe dangerous tranf-
ports!

COUNTESS.

Talk down the tempeft!—laugh away defpair!

YOUNG COUNT.

Thus grov'ling at your feet, I crave for mercy!
Will nothing move!

COUNTESS. (*pointing to his father's body*)

Monfter!—look there!—look there!.

YOUNG COUNT.

Diftra&ing fight! Forgive me! O! forgive!

COUNT OF COLMAR.

How cou'd thy heart be harden'd to infli&
Such dreadful cruelties, on fuch a father!
Who cou'd excite thee to fuch impious condu&?

YOUNG COUNT.

The vile Lapont, by long and various arts!
Bafe as I was to liften to his counfel!—
Wicked as bafe!—work'd up my foul to all!—

COUNTESS.

" Cruel!—unnatural!—what cou'd work thy
heart,

" What arts, what counfel! to fuch deeds of horror!—

" But he has his meed!—The blood whofe tainted
fpots

" Defile that reverend face, fprang from his heart!

" Old as he was, and dying, yet thy father,

" To fave my life, exerted ftrength to kill him!'

YOUNG

YOUNG COUNT.

" Tenfold accurs'd! dar'd he attempt thy life!

COUNTESS.

" Is that a wonder?—Was he not thy tutor?

YOUNG COUNT.

" Alas! he early tempted me to vice!

" Corrupted firft, and then controled my mind.

" Intemp'rate riot, and profufe expence,

" Impell'd, at laft, my father to reprove.

" Again I err'd ; again his fterner voice

" Check'd my career, and threaten'd punifhment.

" Impetuous, headftrong, blinded by my paffions,

" Lapont, affiduous, fann'd my caufelefs rage ;

" Pictur'd my father as a gloomy tyrant,

" And hinted there were means, wou'd I employ
    them,

" To give me full poffeffion of his fortune,"

Ere lingering nature clos'd his eyes in peace.

COUNTESS.

And you cou'd liften to the dangerous villain!

Cou'd calmly liften, and not drive him from you

With execrations !——

YOUNG COUNT.

Curs'd infatuation,

That made me yield my foul to fuch a wretch!

For prefs'd by urgent debts, and urgent vice,

In an ill hour, I follow'd his bafe counfel.

COUNTESS.

" O fatal hour !—Finifh thy horrid tale !

YOUNG COUNT.

" Feigning remorfe to the afflicted Count,

" Reftlefs

" Reftlefs with forrow, forrow for my faults!
" A foporific I adminifter'd,
" Which fimulating death, made all believe,
" All but Lapont and me, my father dead.
" Laid in his coffin, at the dead of night
" We took him thence, and plac'd him in the dun-
       geon,
" Which long difus'd, was only known to us;
" Then fill'd the leaden cafe with mimic weight,
" And foon interr'd it, with funereal pomp,
" In the fame vault where lay his anceftors.—
" By night, when all we thought were faft afleep,
" We us'd to carry him his fcanty food,
" Wretch that I was! And thence the tale of ghofts.
" You know the reft.

MATILDA.
" Alas! we know too much!
" Wou'd I had never heard the dreadful tale!

COLMAR.
O! my dear Montval! what a fate was thine!

YOUNG COUNT.
Yet he forgave! you heard how he forgave!

COUNTESS. (groaning deeply)
Forgave!—But can'ft thou ere forgive thyfelf?

YOUNG COUNT.
Never, while you repulfe me! Let me thus——
       [Offering to take her hand.]

COUNTESS.
Stand off!—avaunt!—Pollute me; touch me
    not!
Look at thy parricid'al hands!—

Think

Think of thy parricid'al heart!— ....
They drop with blood!—with blood!—a father's
    blood!

          YOUNG COUNT.

  Oh! one embrace, and I fhall die content!—

          COUNTESS.

Anguifh! diftraction! Sooner I'd embrace
Deformity and age, and peftilence!
Rather wou'd clafp, within thefe wretched arms,
The loathfome leper, livid from the tomb,
Than taint my breaft with thy abhorr'd endear-
    ments!

          YOUNG COUNT. *(Wildly)*

Then what is left me?—

          COUNTESS.

      Shame! remorfe! defpair!
Fruitlefs repentance, and a lingering death!

       YOUNG COUNT. *(Suddenly ftabbing bimfelf)*

No! this fhall free me from the latter curfe

                    [*Falls.*

          COUNTESS.

Montval! Montval!—O! I have murder'd him!
Murder'd my hufband.

       [*Throwing herfelf down by him.*]

          MATILDA. *(Weeping)*

    " Miferable man!
" O! that my noble friend had never known thee!

          MARQUIS.

  " He is not dead! Bend him a little forward!"

          COUNTESS.

My deareft lord! O yet, if life remains,
O! yet look up and hear me fpeak forgivenefs!
Feel my embrace, and witnefs my defpair!

        I   YOUNG

YOUNG COUNT. *(faintly)*

Can you fpeak thus!—Then I fhall die in peace!
Forgive me, thou Great God! all my offences!
Place me, O place me by my father's fide!
That I may weep over his clay-cold hand,
And figh upon it my laft breath of life!

> [*They move him to his father's body, taking
> whofe hand, and fervently kiffing it,
> he fays.*]

Moft injur'd, moft rever'd! O! may thy fpirit
Plead at th' eternal bar.   [*Dies.*

COUNTESS.

> [*Clafping him clofely in her arms as they try
> to raife her.*]

Hold off! Hold off! for I will die with him.

> [*Swoons in Matilda's arms.*]

MATILDA,

Heart-rending fpectacle! unhappy friend,
Exert your fortitude!

MARQUIS.

She hears you not!
So deadly is the fwoon that locks her fenfes.
Run for fome help to move thefe bodies hence.

> [*To Terefa.*]

Convey the haplefs Countefs to her chamber,
Where let our tender care and friendfhip watch her,
Till time fhall bring his balm to heal her wounded
    mind!

The Curtains drops, and the Play ends.

EPILOGUE,

By the AUTHOR of the TRAGEDY,

AND

SPOKEN BY MRS. POWELL.

GHOST—or *no* ghoft?—For *both* have ftood the teft—
Ghoft or *no* ghoft?—Pray which has pleas'd you beft?
But need I afk? Or can the *Author* wreftle,
With the enchanting ghoft of Conway Caftle?
Tho' kind applaufes hail'd the fancied fprite,
Transform'd into a poor old man to-night,
He dares not hope applaufe fo long, fo clear,
As almoft ftunn'd the fpectre of laft year.
But—*a propos*—pray was it not provoking
To *make* the Countefs—nay! 'tis paft all joking,—
At midnight!—in a dungeon! quite alone!
Brave an hobgoblin, and his hollow groan!—
Dear ladies! I wou'd ftake my life upon it,
That neither *you*,—nor you,—nor YOU had done it!
Nay!—had fome *beaux* I fee, been in *her* place,
Their *hands* had not been *whiter* than their *face.*
For me!—to all the audience be it known—
I hate, and fear *all fpectres*—fave *my own.**
But, hence! the jeft profane!—'Twere impious here,
From the fad eye, to chafe the graceful tear:
No ftudied woes have wak'd the Poet's art,
To touch the tender pulfes of the heart:
No high-wrought fiction mov'd the pitying figh,
For Kings who languifh, or for Queens who cry;
But the real tale of deep domeftic woe,
Has made your bofoms throb, your forrows flow.
Too folemn, then, too *homefelt* is the fcene,
For Epilogue to come with flippant mien,—
And turn to fafhionable Farce a part,
Which thrills the fineft fibres of the heart.
Let thofe who love juft jefting, feek to fhine;
But never may the odious tafk be mine.—

* *Alluding to this Lady's part in the Caftle Spectre.*

M